Summer Sun Risin'

To Ylla and Aaron, for all your dreams
—W.N-L.

I first thank God. This artwork is dedicated to my Aunt Eleanora E. Tate for
her insight and guidance, and for inspiring me to reach beyond the sun
—D.T.

Text copyright © 2002 by W. Nikola-Lisa
Illustrations copyright © 2002 by Don Tate

All rights reserved. No part of the contents of this book may be reproduced
by any means without the written permission of the publisher.
LEE & LOW BOOKS Inc., 95 Madison Avenue, New York, NY 10016
www.leeandlow.com

The artist would like to give special thanks to the Johnson family, Frank, Aretha, and
Shai, who served as models for the characters in this book.

Printed in China

Book design by David Neuhaus/NeuStudio
Book production by The Kids at Our House

The text is set in NeueNeuland.
The illustrations are rendered in oil and acrylic paint on textured Canson paper.

10 9 8 7 6 5 4 3 2 1   First Edition

Library of Congress Cataloging-in-Publication Data
Nikola-Lisa, W.
Summer sun risin' / by W. Nikola-Lisa ; illustrated by Don Tate.— 1st ed.
p. cm.
Summary: An African American boy enjoys a summer day on his family's
farm, milking the cows, fishing, and having fun.
ISBN 1-58430-034-5
[1. Farm life—Fiction. 2. African Americans—Fiction. 3. Stories in rhyme.]
I. Title: Summer sun rising. II. Tate, Don, ill. III. Title.
PZ 8.3.N 5664 Su 2002   [E]—dc 21   2001029720

Summer Sun Risin'

by W. Nikola-Lisa

illustrated by Don Tate

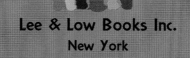

Lee & Low Books Inc.
New York

Wake up, little one—
summer sun's a-risin'!

Rug on the floor,
  light on the wall.
Ma by the bed,
  Pa in the hall.

Dog at the door,
  cat on a chair.
Summer sun's tastin'
  the sweet, sweet air.

Milk in a glass,
egg in a cup.
Toast on a plate
butter side up.

Fritters in a pan,
coffee in the pot.
Summer sun's risin',
makin' it hot.

Birds in the roost,
   kittens in the yarn.
Cows linin' up
   down by the barn.

Pa cracks the door,
   I swing it wide.
Summer sun's shinin',
   floodin' inside.

Chicks in the yard
  scratchin' for seed.
Pigs at the trough
  waitin' to feed.

Pa by the shed
  rollin' out wire.
Summer sun's climbin'
  higher and higher.